KNOW YOUR RIGHTS™

THE JUVENILE COURT SYSTEM

YOUR LEGAL RIGHTS

RICHARD BARRINGTON

ROSEN PUBLISHING
New York

Published in 2016 by The Rosen Publishing Group, Inc.

29 East 21st Street, New York, NY 10010

First Edition

Expert Reviewer: Lindsay A. Lewis, Esq.

Library of Congress Cataloging-in-Publication Data

Barrington, Richard, 1961– author.
The juvenile court system: your legal rights/Richard Barrington.—First edition.
pages cm.—(Know your rights)
Includes bibliographical references and index.
ISBN 978-1-4777-8040-4 (library bound)—
ISBN 978-1-4777-8621-5 (pbk.)—
ISBN 978-1-4994-3678-5 (6-pack)
1. Juvenile justice, Administration of—United States—Juvenile literature. I. Title.
KF9780.B37 2016
345.73'081—dc23

2014035236

Manufactured in the United States of America

For many of the images in this book, the people photographed are models. The depictions do not imply actual situations or events.

CONTENTS

INTRODUCTION

Up until September 2006, Torey Adamcik seemed pretty much like a standard sixteen-year-old high school student. Today, he is serving life in prison without the possibility of parole.

How Torey went from a future of proms, graduation, and college to life behind bars involves the murder of a schoolmate. The case is controversial—a court found him guilty and an appeals court denied him a retrial—but he claims he is innocent, and there is an extensive argument to be made in his favor. Guilty or innocent, his case demonstrates some of the dangers that await juveniles who do not understand juvenile crime and the juvenile justice system.

A number of factors contributed to Torey receiving a life sentence:

- He associated regularly with a classmate who had violent fantasies and an unhealthy fascination with the Columbine High killers.
- Upon his arrest, he spoke to police without an attorney present.
- While not admitting guilt, he made statements that helped prosecutors gain a conviction.
- He stood trial as an adult, not as a juvenile.
- He received ineffective defense representation.

(Note: In 2010, the Supreme Court abolished mandatory life sentences without parole for juveniles. However, in limited circumstances there are still juveniles sentenced to life without parole.)

Many of these pitfalls could have been avoided with a better understanding of the law and the juvenile justice system. This book will help others avoid this kind of fate by explaining some of the basics of the law, how the juvenile court system works, what circumstances often get juveniles in trouble, what rights a juvenile has when arrested, and what consequences a juvenile might face if found guilty of a crime. The primary goal is to help young

When juveniles appear before a court of law, the more they know about how the system works, the better they can protect their rights.

people avoid getting into trouble, and a secondary goal is to show them how to keep any trouble they get into from getting out of hand.

Many of the rights and protections provided in the juvenile justice system stem from the case of a teenager who was arrested more than fifty years ago. Like Torey Adamcik, fifteen-year-old Jerry Gault's problems started by choosing the wrong friend—in this case, someone who liked making obscene phone calls. When Jerry was arrested because he was present when one of these phone calls was made, he was assumed not to have any of the rights normally afforded to adults when they are arrested. He received a six-year sentence.

The case eventually went to the Supreme Court, which overturned the conviction. The Supreme Court's opinion made clear that even though Jerry was a minor, he was still entitled to the basic rights of due process guaranteed under the U.S. Constitution.

The Gault case helped provide juveniles with a series of basic protections under the law. As a practical matter, though, the justice system's first priority is often to prosecute rather than to defend the rights of people who have been arrested. An understanding of what your rights are, and when they apply, will best allow you to exercise those rights when you need to. After reading this book, a young person should be better prepared both to stay out of legal trouble and to handle legal trouble if it comes up.

CHAPTER 1

LEARNING THE SYSTEM

The worst time for teenagers to start to learn about the juvenile court system is when they find themselves in trouble. At that point, they may find out that what they don't know can definitely hurt them.

This is not to say the juvenile court system is the enemy of young people. In a way, it is just the opposite—it is a special branch of the U.S. justice system that is designed to meet the needs and circumstances of people who are old enough to have violated the law, but who may not yet be old enough to fully understand the meaning and consequences of their actions.

For better or worse, juvenile courts are part of a system, and like any system, this one has rules and procedures. The more a person understands about how the system works, the better that person will be able to protect his or her rights and interests. The following is a look at some of the basics of that system.

WHO IS CONSIDERED A JUVENILE?

The word "juvenile" is used generally to describe someone who is physically or psychologically not yet fully mature. From a legal standpoint, it applies to people who fall under the jurisdiction of the juvenile court system. This means that they will be subject to different procedures and penalties than someone being tried as an adult.

Of course, the definition of what it means to be fully mature is a matter of opinion, so each state defines a specific age at which a person is no longer considered a juvenile. This age varies from state to state, but in most states eighteen is the magic number—in those states, an eighteen-year-old accused of a crime will be tried as an adult. In some states, though, sixteen- or seventeen-year-olds are tried as adults.

Whatever the age limit in a given state, sometimes the nature and circumstances of a crime are such that even someone within the age range for juvenile court can be tried as an adult.

STRUCTURE OF THE JUVENILE COURT SYSTEM

One of the challenges in understanding the juvenile court system is that it varies from state to state. However, there are similarities in the different stages of the process, so the upcoming section on case flow will help make sense of what happens when one is brought before any court within the juvenile court system. First, though, the following are some of the key variables that will determine where that process takes place and who makes the decisions:

Jurisdiction: The justice system is made up of local, state, and federal jurisdictions, and most crimes involving juveniles are determined according to state laws. Some states

The specific court juveniles appear before depends on the nature of the accusation and the laws and practices of the state.

leave it to local courts (such as a county or town court) to handle juvenile violations, while others use state courts for this purpose.

Processing: Some jurisdictions have special courts set up for juveniles, while others rely on their normal court systems to try juvenile cases. In either case, anyone being tried as a juvenile is subject to the same special laws and protections provided to juveniles.

Type of violation: The type of court into which a juvenile will be brought might also depend on what the charge against him or her is. If there is not an important distinction between how an adult or a juvenile would be processed (as with routine traffic violations, for example) a juvenile case may go through the same venue that anybody else's would.

In short, the type of court juveniles face depends on what they did and where they did it. However, there are some similarities in the major stages of the system.

CASE FLOW

If all the variables from state to state seem confusing, it should come as no surprise—with fifty states and a huge range of laws on the books, there is an almost limitless number of possible combinations of circumstances. However, it all becomes a little easier to understand when thought of as a step-by-step process. Seeing the way a case flows through the juvenile justice system provides some idea of what to expect.

STATE VS. FEDERAL DISTINCTIONS

A juvenile standing trial is likely to be under state or local jurisdiction rather than in federal court, but, even so, there are standard protections under federal law that apply to all juvenile cases. The following are some of the key areas of difference from state to state, each of which has some common ground rooted in federal law:

- **Body of Law:** Except in rare cases where a juvenile is accused of a federal crime, most offenses are governed by state or local laws. However, one common denominator is that all juveniles are entitled to the same type of due process as adults, which includes representation by counsel unless waived.
- **Waiver of Counsel:** Waiver of counsel—which means giving up the right to have legal representation in criminal proceedings—is one of the riskiest decisions any defendant can make. While federal law guarantees everyone the right to counsel, some states make it easier than others for a juvenile to waive this right. For example, in some states, a judge simply has to advise a juvenile defendant of the right to legal representation, and then that juvenile can waive that right. In many states, a parent or an attorney has to be consulted before a juvenile can waive the right to counsel, while at the most protective end of the scale, some states have outright prohibitions against a juvenile waiving this right, at least in some circumstances. The best thing to remember is that the right to counsel is there for the defendant's protection, so it is almost always best not to waive that right.
- **Purpose of the system:** There is a wide difference in how various states define the purpose of their juvenile justice systems. In some cases, the purpose is strictly

(continued on the next page)

(continued from the previous page)

to protect the community from future offenses. In many cases, though, states call on their juvenile court systems to balance the needs of the community with the development of the young people who pass through those systems. In the most protective states, courts actually have the mandate to assume the role of parent once a juvenile has been removed from the parent's care and placed in the juvenile court system. This can make a difference in whether there are sentencing options designed to rehabilitate or retrain an offender or only those designed to punish and confine the offender.

Step-by-step, here are the major stages in this process:

1. **Intake:** When a juvenile is arrested, the police make an initial decision on how to pursue the matter. Often, a public prosecutor and juvenile authorities might be consulted. The result can range from dropping the case to bringing formal charges, though there is also a middle ground known as diversion. Diversion might consist of an informal remedy to the situation, such as having the juvenile perform community service or participate in counseling.
2. **Detention hearing:** If formal charges are being pursued, there will be a hearing to determine whether the defendant needs to be held in jail or can be released (possibly after posting bail as an assurance of returning to court when ordered).
3. **Preliminary hearing:** A preliminary hearing is a crucial part of the process because it is when a judge decides where and how the case will be pursued. At this stage, the judge could decide to dismiss the charges, but at the other extreme, the judge could decide the juvenile defendant needs

to be tried as an adult. Most often, any formal hearing or trial will be according to the state's juvenile justice procedures.

4. **Adjudication:** This is the formal trial or hearing at which the defendant's guilt or innocence is decided. In juvenile court, a judge listens to both sides, then considers the circumstances and the juvenile's past record in deciding the likelihood of guilt or innocence.

5. **Disposition:** If a juvenile defendant is found guilty, the judge has a wide variety of outcomes to choose from. These may be focused on simply trying to improve

Hearings that take place before a formal trial occurs can be as important to the outcome of the case as the trial itself.

the juvenile's future behavior, but in serious cases the juvenile may be sentenced to a juvenile detention facility.

LEGAL BASICS: INFRACTIONS, MISDEMEANORS, AND FELONIES

As a case flows through the juvenile justice system, there are several paths it can take at each stage of the process. For a juvenile who runs into trouble, the outcomes can range from having the matter dropped almost immediately, to standing trial and being punished as an adult. Most outcomes fall somewhere in between, and where they fall depends on the seriousness of the offense.

When a person is charged with breaking the law, one of the most important things to determine is whether the offense is considered an infraction, a misdemeanor, or a felony. Here is an explanation of the three:

Infractions are minor offenses punishable only by a fine, not by imprisonment. A routine speeding ticket would be an example of an infraction. Infractions are also referred to as violations. They are notable because they are not considered crimes and will be sealed immediately even if a juvenile is found to have committed one. Accordingly, if a juvenile has a violation on record but has never been convicted of a misdemeanor or a felony, he or she would answer no to the question "Have you ever been convicted of a crime?"

Misdemeanors are criminal offenses punishable by less than a year in prison. For example, in most cases, graffitiing would be considered a misdemeanor.

Felonies are crimes that can be punishable by more than a year in prison. These generally involve serious bodily harm or substantial theft or damage of property. Although juveniles charged with a felony might face lesser penalties than adults, it is when charged with a felony that a juvenile runs the greatest risk of being tried as an adult and along with it the greatest risk of imprisonment.

In addition to these standard types of legal offenses, juveniles should be aware of a special category of crime that applies only to people who are not of legal age. These are called status offenses, and they include things such as truancy or curfew violations. In addition, in some states, such as New York, there is a special category of disposition for those offenders between the ages of sixteen and nineteen. Those in this area considered to be between childhood and adulthood can be adjudged youthful offenders by the court at sentencing, which will relieve them of a criminal record even if tried in adult state or federal court and found guilty of a felony offense.

EMERGING TRENDS AND ISSUES

The juvenile justice system has gone through changes over the years, and it is still changing. Here are some of the key issues that are shaping this system in the twenty-first century:

- Overcrowding
- Rapid increase of the juvenile population in some states
- The steady rise in single-parent families

An ordinary traffic ticket would be considered an infraction, which is less serious legally than a misdemeanor or a felony.

- Budget limitations
- Treatment of violent versus nonviolent offenders
- Racial disparity in arrest and conviction rates
- Debate over punishment versus rehabilitation
- Whether and how to make families pay for the cost of detaining juveniles

Often, these issues boil down to debates about effectiveness and money. For anyone encountering the

Overcrowding is a growing problem for the juvenile justice system.

juvenile justice system, it is important to remember that while that system may be there in part to protect young people, there are often financial limits on how much service the system can provide. That is why it is important for young people to know how the system works, so they can insist on the protections and rights to which they are entitled.

CHAPTER 2

FROM FUN AND GAMES TO SERIOUS TROUBLE

Things tend to happen fast for teenagers. Emotions—from lust to greed to anger—rise quickly. Temptations are everywhere, and pressures to please parents, do well in school, and impress peers can be very stressful.

Because there is so much going on in their lives, it can seem to teenagers as though they went from having an ordinary day to being in trouble with the law in the blink of an eye. The real problem is, while trouble can happen in a flash, the consequences can last a lifetime.

This chapter will look at some of the circumstances that often lead to trouble and the consequences that result.

WHAT IS THE PROFILE OF A TYPICAL JUVENILE OFFENDER?

Stereotypes are dangerous things, and they can be especially harmful in discussions of criminal activity. Stereotypes can lead to unfair racial profiling by police and incorrect perceptions on the part of juveniles about who is likely to get into trouble.

For example, it would be easy to oversimplify the profile of the typical juvenile offender as male, black, and living in an urban area. However, not only are there many

For teenagers, even ordinary social situations can quickly turn confrontational or into occasions for trouble.

exceptions to these generalizations, but the face of juvenile crime has been changing over time.

Males do indeed commit most juvenile offenses, but arrest rates among males have dropped sharply in recent decades, while arrest rates among females have stayed fairly level. As a result, the gap between male and female arrest rates has narrowed for both violent and property crimes, but especially for property crimes.

Similar trends describe the relationship between arrest rates for white and black juveniles. Black arrest rates are higher, but the gap has narrowed in recent decades. Fortunately, juvenile violent crime arrest rates for both blacks and whites have declined since peaking in the mid-1990s, with arrest rates falling faster for black juveniles than for white juveniles. The gap in arrest rates between white and black juveniles has also fallen for property crimes.

No group of teenagers should feel that juvenile crime might not be a factor in their lives because of race, gender, or location. Crimes happen in both poor ghettos and rich suburbs and are committed by people of both sexes and all races. A look at the numbers and types of juvenile crimes that are committed will demonstrate that the crimes themselves also come in all varieties.

NUMBERS AND TYPES OF JUVENILE CASES

Some people think getting into a little trouble is just part of growing up, and certainly some crimes committed by

Theft is the most common reason for juvenile arrests.

juveniles are relatively harmless. However, there are also a significant number of more serious crimes committed by juveniles—crimes that have a lasting impact on the people who committed them, as well as their victims.

Of the 1.6 million juvenile arrests made in 2010, the most common category was for larceny/theft. The frequency of larceny/theft arrests should be a warning. These crimes often result from a moment's temptation—a teenager sees the latest pair of Nikes in a store that does not seem closely watched, or perhaps a classmate has left an iPad unattended for a few minutes. These crimes may seem easy to commit, but the numbers say they often result in getting caught.

Other prominent categories of juvenile crime include assault, illegal drug use, disorderly conduct, and liquor law violations. Among violent crimes, aggravated assault (which involves inflicting serious bodily harm) is most common. Fortunately, murder represented less than 1 percent of juvenile crimes, but that is still enough to represent about a thousand lives being taken and another thousand lives being permanently sidetracked by an arrest for a serious crime.

SCHOOL POLICING

Since young people spend much of their time in school, it is not surprising that school is a frequent venue for juvenile crime. In the mid-1980s, a Supreme Court decision in the case of *New Jersey v. T.L.O.* established that in the interest of safety, school officials do not have to meet normal standards of probable cause before searching students and their possessions. Since then, high-profile incidents of school violence have led to a heightened police presence in many schools, with searching and surveillance becoming more and more routine. Some districts have even taken responsibility for school safety away from the principal and turned it over to the local police department.

Students should understand that bringing dangerous or illegal materials to school greatly increases their chances of getting arrested. The overwhelming policy trend is that public safety is a higher priority than individual privacy where schools are concerned, so students should always act on the assumption that their actions will be watched and their possessions searched.

This level of surveillance may be unwelcome and uncomfortable, but it is a reality. A positive effect, though, is that it does cut down on the opportunities for students to get themselves and others in trouble.

Police and school officials have been given broad latitude to search student possessions within schools.

THE COMPANY YOU KEEP

Outside of school, a normal day in the company of other students can turn into trouble for a teen. In fact, juveniles are most likely to commit a violent crime at 3 PM on school days—around the time when they have just gotten out of school but are still around other students.

Besides gangs or other groups intent on illegal activity, just a normal course of conversation among young people can lead to breaking the law—an argument can lead to a fight, a show-off may egg others on to tag a building with graffiti, or physical attraction may lead to unwanted sexual contact.

People often do not do their best thinking in groups. The feeling of shared responsibility can make people in the group take risks they would not ordinarily take, and peer pressure also plays a role. In those situations, a young person needs to think beyond the moment and weigh whether the activity is worth the consequences. This may mean attempting to be the voice of reason in keeping others from doing something they regret, but at the very least it may mean walking away to avoid trouble.

NUMBER OF CONVICTIONS

According to the U.S. Department of Justice, as of 2010, roughly two-thirds of all juveniles who were arrested received some form of punishment. The most common form of punishment is probation, which is an agreement to meet certain rules of behavior and have activity monitored by a probation official.

Only eighty-two out of every one thousand juvenile cases resulted in some form of detention or required placement outside of the home. However, one out of every five juvenile delinquency cases results in detention at some stage of the process, such as while the case is moving through the system.

In terms of the eventual outcome of juvenile cases, between the extremes of dismissal of the case and incarceration are a variety of other sanctions, including probation, fines, paying for damages done, and community service.

The time just after school is when juvenile crime is most likely to occur.

RACIAL DISPARITY IN ARRESTS

Location, time of day, and the company a person keeps can all factor into the likelihood of getting arrested. Unfortunately, so can race. Of the US population between the ages of ten and seventeen, 76 percent is white, but only 66 percent of juveniles arrested are white. This means that members of other races tend to be arrested more frequently compared with their percentage of the population, and this is especially true of African Americans.

While just less than 13 percent of the U.S. population is African American, 33 percent of juveniles arrested for property crimes and 51 percent of juveniles arrested for violent crimes are African American. In other words, the African American population represents more than its share of juvenile arrests, and this is made worse by the fact that African American juveniles who are arrested are more likely than the average juvenile to have their cases go to court, be referred to adult court, and result in long-term prison sentences.

Experts debate whether these out-of-proportion arrest figures are because there is a bias among the police and the courts against African American youth or if the poorer neighborhoods that blacks are more likely to live in lead to a greater temptation for crime. The answer may involve a bit of both, but from the standpoint of any juvenile, African American or otherwise, the important thing to remember is that there are ways of avoiding these pitfalls.

It is especially important for young people whose circumstances are more likely to lead to arrest to be aware of staying out of situations that lead to trouble. If trouble should happen, it then becomes very important to keep in mind how the juvenile justice system works so that a juvenile who has been arrested can get all the rights and protections the law makes available.

It is rare that cases are referred out of juvenile court and into criminal court—this happens with just four out of every one thousand juvenile cases. However, violent crimes are about seven times more likely to be sent to criminal court and are more than twice as likely to result in detention or another form of placement outside of the home.

In short, being arrested usually has consequences. Those consequences are most likely to be administered through the juvenile court system, which is why it is a good idea to know a little about that system. Juveniles who commit more serious crimes, though, may face the higher stakes of trial in criminal court.

HARSHNESS OF PENALTIES

What is the worst that can happen when a juvenile is arrested? While the juvenile court system is designed to take into account the special needs and circumstances of people who have not yet reached adulthood, being a juvenile does not get a person off the hook for illegal behavior.

In 2010, there were nearly seventy-one thousand juveniles in the United States who were in residential placement facilities. This means that these juveniles were in one form of custody or other, such as prisons and mental health facilities. The most common reason these seventy-one thousand juveniles were placed in those facilities was because of violent crimes.

For more serious crimes, the consequences can be much longer lasting. There are more than two thousand people in U.S. prisons serving life sentences without parole for crimes they committed as juveniles. In more than half

As of 2010, more than seventy thousand U.S. juveniles were in some form of custody for crimes they had committed.

these cases, the crime in question was their first offense. One of the main harms caused by transfer to adult court is that while a juvenile record is sealed, an adult record can haunt you for the rest of your life: when applying for jobs, when seeking financial aid for higher education, when attempting to enlist in the military or applying to work for law enforcement. It can prevent your eligibility for government assistance, and it can threaten your immigration status if you are in the United States illegally or are not a permanent resident. Thus, in general, possible incarceration is not the only consequence of criminal behavior. Your conduct can affect you long after you are out of the system and pursuing your life and career goals.

CHAPTER 3

WHAT TO DO IF YOU ARE ARRESTED AS A JUVENILE

The juvenile justice system can seem a little overwhelming, but no teenager has to know all the details in order to survive that system. In fact, more important than knowing about the system for people who have been arrested is knowing how to handle themselves.

For starters, keep in mind three simple goals:

1. Do not take the blame for anything you did not do.
2. Minimize the potential consequences of what you did do.
3. Do not add to the problem by making more mistakes.

The following sections will give some insight into how to accomplish those goals.

KNOW YOUR RIGHTS

The juvenile justice system is designed to protect the rights of young people, but it is also there to punish those who commit crimes. People who work in that system are sometimes more focused on the punishment part of the job than protecting rights, so a juvenile entering the system has to be prepared to stand up for his or her own rights. The first step in doing that is to know those rights.

Knowing how to act if arrested can help minimize the consequences of the arrest.

When a person is arrested, one of the officers involved should read the suspect what are known as Miranda rights. Anyone who has grown up watching crime shows on television can probably recite most of the Miranda rights by heart. They begin with, "You have the right to remain silent."

The Miranda rights are important, but they are not the only rights a juvenile has in the justice system. Here are some key rights to remember if you are arrested:

- **The right to a phone call.** Calling your parents, assuming they are reliable, is the best way to use this right. A good alternative is a trusted adult who can help look out for your interests.
- **The right to remain silent.** The authorities most likely will try to lure you into saying something. The trick is actually remaining silent.
- **The right to an attorney.** Until an attorney is provided, the best approach is to say nothing other than to keep insisting on your right to see a lawyer.
- **The right to avoid self-incrimination.** At no stage of the process, either before or during trial, are you required to make any statement that would help prove you committed a crime.
- **The right to be informed of charges.** A suspect is supposed to be informed of the charges being made in advance of having to stand trial on those charges.
- **The right to a trial.** In juvenile court, this will probably be a trial decided by a judge rather than a jury.
- **The right to appeal.** This does not mean defendants get a "do-over" if they do not like their case, but it does mean that they have a right to challenge the proceedings, including the final disposition and sentencing if they can demonstrate that their rights were violated or the law was not properly applied. This right can also be applied in limited circumstances if a defendant has pled guilty. Defendants should consult an attorney to determine if there are any viable grounds for appeal and should make sure to preserve their right to

If arrested, juveniles should insist on their right to consult with an attorney.

appeal, through their attorney, at every stage.

Insisting on these rights will help juveniles avoid being found guilty of crimes they did not commit and will help limit the consequences of crimes they did commit.

WHAT TO DO AND HOW TO ACT

Knowing your rights is the first step. Standing up for those rights without making further trouble is the next. Here are some tips:

1. **Make a mental note of everything.**

Observing everything, such as whether the police read the Miranda rights, how long it took to see an attorney, and what conditions were like while being detained, may prove to be very important.

2. **Be respectful.** While it may be important not to cooperate by discussing the situation, there is nothing to be gained by annoying the people in charge.

3. **Ask what the charge is.** Police can bring someone in without charging him or her with a crime, but in order to hold someone for any length of time, they have to make a formal charge. Asking whether you are free to leave will indicate whether or not you are under arrest.

4. **Don't answer any questions until an attorney is present.** Until that time, simply respond to any question by saying, "I am exercising my right to remain silent and my right to an attorney."

5. **Explain the situation to the attorney calmly and clearly.** An attorney may have a limited amount of time for interviewing a suspect, so the more quickly you can come to the point, the better.

6. **Speak only in the presence of the attorney.** After your attorney has left, the authorities may try once again to get new information out of you. Having discussed the case with an attorney does not mean it is a good idea to talk to anyone else about it.

7. **State only the bare facts.** Speculating, offering opinions, or saying anything that can be disputed can make it seem as though a person is not telling the truth.

8. **Do not lie.** Doing so can open you up to charges such as obstructing a police investigation or perjury, which can have more serious consequences than

SEEKING LEGAL REPRESENTATION

A juvenile who has just been arrested for the first time probably has no experience with hiring an attorney. Whether the court appoints one or the juvenile or his or her family is in a position to hire one, here are some questions that can help determine the attorney's qualifications:

- How much experience do you have defending juveniles?
- How much experience do you have with the types of charges in this case?
- What is your caseload, and how much time do you have to spend on this case?
- Have you ever been the subject of a professional complaint or disciplinary action against you as an attorney?
- What do you think is the best defense strategy in this case?
- What possible punishments might result from a guilty verdict?
- What do you think the most likely outcome is?
- What outcomes have you gotten in similar cases?

Asking these questions can accomplish two things. It can help screen out anyone who is clearly unsuited to the job. It can also put the attorney on notice that the juvenile defendant is actively engaged in the process and worthy of a thorough effort.

Juveniles should also make sure that their attorneys understand what is at stake for them. They should inform their attorneys of their life and career goals, as well as their U.S. citizenship status. This information helps attorneys decide how to mitigate collateral consequences (consequences that go beyond the specific sentence for the crime), which in many situations can be worse than the actual punishment for the crime itself.

the original accusation. It is better to say nothing at all.

CHILDHOOD'S END: BEING TRIED AS AN ADULT

The juvenile court system offers several protections for someone who has been accused of a crime. Sentences are often limited and in some cases are ended as soon as the person reaches the age twenty-one. In general, the approach of juvenile courts is to encourage rehabilitation rather than focus simply on punishing wrongdoers. Juvenile conviction records have a greater degree of confidentiality than adult records, which helps juveniles make a fresh start once they reach adulthood.

Unfortunately, being a juvenile does not guarantee being tried in juvenile court. Some states give prosecutors the option of bypassing juvenile court and filing a case directly in criminal court. Certain serious crimes are required to be tried in criminal court in some states. There is not much that juveniles who have been arrested can do about those situations, but those realities are a reminder that committing more serious crimes can result in losing the special protections usually given to juveniles.

Even cases that start out in juvenile court may wind up in criminal court. Juvenile court judges have the option of transferring cases to criminal court if they think the situation demands it. This is one of many reasons why it is important to retain legal counsel as soon as possible—this transfer decision is made in a preliminary hearing, before the case is tried.

Finally, one more reason for avoiding transfer to

For serious crimes, even youthful offenders may find themselves tried in criminal courts.

criminal court is that most states require that once a juvenile has been transferred to criminal court, they must automatically be tried in criminal court for all future offenses. Legally and otherwise, a transfer to criminal court can force juveniles to grow up before they are ready.

HOW DO YOU PLEAD? OPTIONS AND CONSEQUENCES

When a case goes to trial, the accused has the choice of

pleading guilty or not guilty. However, even before trial, a person under arrest might be offered a variety of deals that are the same as pleading guilty. It is important to recognize all the options and implications in those situations. There are basically two options. The first is take a deal by which the accused pleads guilty, often in the hopes or with the promise of some leniency by the court, such as a reduced sentence, which might in many cases include placement in a program or some alternative to incarceration. The other option is to proceed to trial, in which case a judge will find the defendant either guilty or not guilty of the offenses charged.

As noted previously, the most common form of punishment for juvenile offenders is probation. Probation—which can be thought of as getting off with a warning—might seem like a convenient way to avoid all the trouble of getting an attorney and seeing a case through trial, especially if the juvenile is being detained while awaiting trial or a hearing. However, accepting probation means admitting to having committed the offense, and that can have long-term consequences. The terms of probation often include a series of conditions, the violation of which can result in harsher consequences, including detention.

To start with, it is important to determine whether the charge in question is an infraction, a misdemeanor, or a felony. If it is simply an infraction, admitting guilt typically means nothing more than paying a fine or making restitution in some form. However, if the charge is a misdemeanor or a felony, those are criminal charges that could impact eligibility for student loans, military service, public housing, or certain types of employment. In short, even if the immediate

Deciding how to plead may be the most important decision you have to make after being arrested.

punishment is not severe, pleading guilty can have a negative impact on a person's life.

Clearly then, pleading guilty or accepting any kind of a deal should be done only after consulting with an attorney. Even then, the accused should consider what is being offered in return—not just in terms of the immediate punishment, but in terms of long-term impact.

CHAPTER 4

OWNING THE CONSEQUENCES

Since most juveniles who are arrested receive some form of punishment, some thought should be given to how to handle legal punishment once it has been handed out.

The goals should be to get through the punishment without making conditions any worse than they have to be and, most of all, to learn from the experience to avoid repeating behaviors that led to the punishment in the first place.

LIVING WITH PROBATION

As noted previously, probation is the most common form of punishment given to juvenile offenders. While probation allows a fair amount of freedom, there are responsibilities that come with that freedom.

A juvenile on probation can typically resume normal activities such as going to school and work. However, he or she must regularly meet with a probation officer and may be subject to a variety of other conditions. These conditions may include following a curfew, performing community service, making restitution for damage done, and attending substance abuse counseling.

The responsibilities involved are twofold: one is to meet the conditions set forth under the probation terms. The other is to make sure the freedom granted does not lead to the commission of new offenses. A juvenile who violates

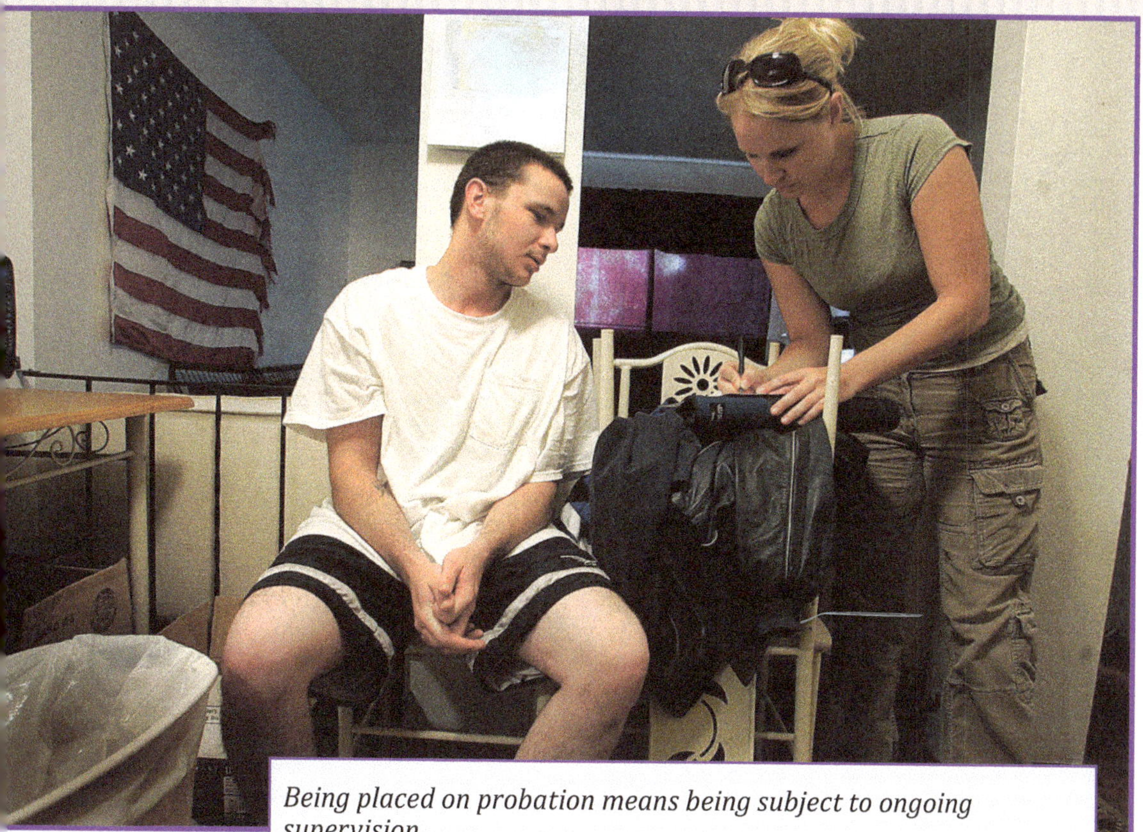

Being placed on probation means being subject to ongoing supervision.

probation faces having the original case returned to the court, where more serious penalties will be considered. He or she also is less likely to receive such leniency for future offenses.

JUVENILE CORRECTION FACILITIES

Although probation is the most common option for juvenile offenders, repeat offenders or those who commit more serious offenses can be placed in some sort of custody. This

Group homes are one of the custody options for juvenile offenders.

does not necessarily involve going to what would traditionally be thought of as jail—roughly four out of ten juveniles in custody as of 2010 were in that type of facility. Other common custody options are group homes and residential treatment centers.

While sentencing may require that a juvenile essentially live at the facility, in many cases, residents may have some freedom of movement during the day, and a little fewer than half of juvenile correction facilities lock their residents up at night.

Juveniles who want to avoid further trouble should have two goals in mind while confined to a correctional facility. One is to stay out of trouble. Being in those facilities means living in close quarters with people of similar age and a variety of attitudes. There will be temptations to engage in criminal activities, as well as disagreements that could lead to confrontations. To avoid turning a short sentence into a long one, it is important to walk away from both kinds of situations.

The second goal should be to benefit from the improvement opportunities the facility offers. These can

Juvenile custody facilities often offer skills training, which can be an opportunity for young offenders to improve their lives after they are released.

come in the form of rehabilitation, mental health counseling, skills training, or education. Of the juvenile corrections facilities in the United States, 92 percent report that some or all of their residents attend some form of schooling. Certainly, being sentenced to custody of any sort is a serious form of punishment. However, the system is designed to provide opportunities along with that punishment, so the smartest way to spend time in such a facility is by making maximum use of those opportunities.

GETTING YOUR LIFE BACK AFTER A CONVICTION

The consequences of being convicted of a crime or pleading guilty to one do not end once the probationary period or custody sentence is over. Having a record—even a juvenile record—can affect employment opportunities for the rest of a person's life.

There are a great many jobs that have the discretion to bar someone who has been guilty of crimes in the past, and some are required to ban those people. The American Bar Association has put together a website to show the collateral consequences of committing a crime. This website, www.abacollateralconsequences.org, lists hundreds of occupations that may restrict prior offenders under federal law, and on top of that, individual states have their own restrictions.

While too many specific jobs can be restricted to list here, there are three broad themes to the types of restrictions:

The more serious the crime, the more it restricts employment opportunities. A felony is much more likely to bar someone from a job than a misdemeanor, but even a misdemeanor can get a person excluded from some jobs.

The type of crime may restrict a person from related jobs. For example, someone with a conviction for fraud may not be allowed to work in jobs involving financial responsibility.

A criminal conviction can affect employment opportunities for the rest of a person's life.

Drug offenses can be especially limiting. Federal drug-free workplace requirements mean some organizations that receive financial assistance from the government may be restricted from employing people who have committed drug offenses.

These ongoing consequences are important considerations when deciding how best to resolve a case, and they are also reasons why the distinction between a felony, a misdemeanor, and a violation can be crucial. Most of all, though, these restrictions should be additional reasons to avoid committing a crime in the first place.

CLEARING A JUVENILE RECORD

Wait a minute: how can crimes committed as a juvenile have lifelong consequences, such as limiting employment? Isn't one of the protections of the juvenile justice system that juvenile records are kept confidential? The confidentiality of juvenile records is greatly overstated. It does have some basis in reality, but there are many exceptions. Here are three:

1. Juvenile records are kept confidential only if the juvenile applies to have the record expunged (destroyed or sealed) upon reaching age eighteen. Typically, a probation officer can help with this. Records will not automatically be expunged if the juvenile does not apply for it to happen. If the record is not expunged, the juvenile is required to answer yes when asked about a prior record, which commonly happens on employment, financial aid, and licensing applications.
2. Convictions in adult court remain on the record. This highlights the importance of the preliminary hearing in which a judge may decide to transfer a case to criminal court and why it is important for the juvenile to have legal representation at this early stage of the process.
3. Some applications, such as those for military service, require full disclosure of all prior offenses, even those committed as a juvenile and even if the record has been expunged.

In addition to these technical exceptions to the confidentiality of juvenile records, some privacy advocates are concerned that with the growing drive to create electronic databases of all arrest records, it will become increasingly difficult to wipe the slate clean of prior offenses.

RECOGNIZING RISK FACTORS

Finding constructive educational or employment opportunities is one way to stay out of further trouble after you have been punished for a crime; recognizing and avoiding situations that lead to trouble is also key.

Here are some situations to avoid:

Hanging around after school. As mentioned previously, juveniles are most prone to committing crimes right after school, so getting home or to an organized activity as soon as possible is a good idea.

Being out late at night. Trouble often happens late at night—temptations are many, and people are often tired or feeling the effects of drugs or alcohol.

Association with troublemakers. Some people just do not care about their own futures or about anyone else around them. It is best not to spend time with people like this since they attract trouble.

Occasions where rivals meet. It may be gangs facing off, or it may be at a sporting event between two nearby schools, but when groups of young people with something to prove

Finding employment can be a good way of staying out of trouble while earning an income.

meet up, trouble often results.

The use of intoxicants. Drugs and alcohol can dull people's judgment and make them violent. Even juveniles who resist using intoxicants themselves would be better off not being around those who do.

Being around firearms. Two things can result from being around illegal firearms, both of them bad: a person could be charged with a crime, or a person could be shot.

Often, trouble happens so quickly it is hard to pull away from it once it has started. The safest thing is to walk away as soon as you recognize the type of situation that leads to trouble.

MANAGING RISK FACTORS

"Recidivism" is a technical term for getting back into trouble after having served a sentence for a prior offense. Unfortunately, recidivism rates tend to be quite high, especially for younger people. A U.S. Department of Justice study found that 67.5 percent of people who were released from prison were arrested again within three years. That rearrest rate jumps to 79.9 percent for people under twenty-one.

On the positive side, juvenile arrest rates have been trending downward over the past couple decades. Most juveniles never get arrested, and more and more are succeeding in staying out of trouble. Here are some guidelines that can help someone manage the risk factors that tend to get young people in trouble:

Know the rules. From curfews to laws about alcohol and drug possession, be aware of your community's laws, especially those specific to juveniles.

Have a plan for each day. A person should plan exactly what to do when leaving school, whether it is heading for an organized activity or home to take care of schoolwork. Just waiting around for something to do often turns into waiting for trouble.

Set long-term goals. Whether it is college, getting a job, or starting a family, a focus on positive long-term goals helps a person understand what he might be giving up if he gives in to temptation.

Respect yourself. People are often drawn into trouble by intimidation or loneliness. The more confidence and pride young people have, the better they will understand that their futures are too valuable to let others ruin them.

By following these guidelines, a young person who has been arrested previously can beat the odds of recidivism

GANG RECRUITMENT OF JUVENILES

One thing that makes it tough for young people to stay out of trouble is that gangs are constantly trying to pull in new recruits. Even adult gangs try to attract juveniles, for good reason—juveniles can often be bullied into taking the risk for illegal activities and do not ask as much in return as adult members. As a result, roughly two out of every five gang members are adults.

While gang activity is often associated with inner cities, gangs have also been reported in suburbs, small towns, and rural areas. While cities are more likely to have gangs, juveniles typically make up a bigger portion of gang members outside cities than those in cities. So, gangs can be a challenge for young people no matter where they live.

This challenge is widespread. As of 2010, it was estimated that there were nearly thirty thousand gangs in the United States, totaling about 750 thousand members. These gangs are a persistent source of danger to themselves and those around them. While violent crime has generally declined throughout the United States over the past several years, gang-related violent crime has not seen a similar drop-off.

It is important to remember that when a gang recruits a juvenile, it is not for the juvenile's benefit. Often, it is so the gang can benefit at the expense of the juvenile. As dangerous as it can seem to say no to a gang, saying yes usually turns out to be far more dangerous.

and avoid future trouble. Even better, juveniles who have not been in trouble in the past have the odds of staying out of trouble on their side, and following these guidelines can further improve their chances.

CONCLUSION

On the one hand, the juvenile justice system is designed to protect people who have not yet reached adulthood. On the other hand, juveniles have been sentenced to life in prison without parole, so those protections are not absolute.

Knowing how the system works, from the laws behind it to the punishments that can result from it, can help a young person make decisions that make a big difference—from choosing to stay out of trouble in the first place to minimizing consequences if he or she does get in trouble.

The general idea young people should understand about the juvenile justice system is that it serves two purposes: one is to look after the special needs of young people, but the other is to prosecute those who have been accused of crimes. In short, the system is at times both a friend and an adversary.

Getting the most out of the protections the system is designed to provide depends on knowing what those protections are and how to insist on them. Next to avoiding trouble in the first place, knowledge can be a person's best defense.

GLOSSARY

attorney Someone trained in the law who is licensed to practice law within a given state or states.

collateral consequence An impact of being found guilty of a crime, such as being prohibited from holding certain types of jobs, that goes beyond the specific sentence for the crime.

criminal court A court where a juvenile might be sent instead of juvenile court to be tried as an adult when suspected of committing a serious crime.

diversion An alternative to sending a juvenile case to court, this is generally an attempt to correct the wrongdoing, such as by having the accused make restitution or attend counseling.

expunged In a legal sense, this means effectively wiping a record clean by having it either sealed or destroyed.

felony A crime punishable by a year or more in prison.

group home A facility where people, such as juvenile offenders, can live together under supervised conditions but without the full restrictions of prison.

infraction A noncriminal violation of the law, such as a routine traffic violation.

jurisdiction An area in which a particular group of laws and judicial oversight prevails.

juvenile A person deemed by law not to have reached adulthood.

Miranda rights The basic rights of someone who has been arrested, such as the right to remain silent, which police in the United States are obligated to read to a person upon arrest.

misdemeanor A criminal offense punishable by less than a year in prison.

plead The formal response to a criminal charge, which is usually either guilty or innocent.

probation A type of criminal sentence in which the person is free to go home, but remains under the supervision of the court and is subject to further punishment if specified conditions are violated.

recidivism A repetition of, or relapse into, criminal behavior.

rehabilitate In a legal sense, this means to teach someone to refrain from future criminal behavior.

residential placement facility Any facility where criminal violators may be held while serving their sentences. This can range from a prison to a group home.

residential treatment center A facility where criminal violators may be held for the specific purpose of providing them with counseling to address problems such as addiction or mental health issues.

status offense Behavior that is only a violation of the law when done by a juvenile, such as violating an age-specific curfew or truancy.

waiver of counsel A defendant voluntarily giving up the right to legal representation in criminal proceedings.

FOR MORE INFORMATION

Center on Juvenile and Criminal Justice
40 Boardman Place
San Francisco, CA 94103
(415) 621-5661
Website: http://www.cjcj.org
This independent, nonprofit organization that provides services, technical assistance, and policy analysis designed to reduce the use of incarceration as a solution to society's problems.

Government of Canada Department of Justice
284 Wellington Street
Ottawa, ON K1A 0H8
Canada
(613) 957-4222
Website: http://www.justice.gc.ca
This branch of the Canadian government oversees law enforcement, with a website providing information on a wide range of legal issues, including youth justice.

Justice for Youth and Children
Canadian Foundation for Children, Youth and the Law
415 Yonge Street, Suite 1203
Toronto, ON M5B 2E7
Canada
Website: http://www.jfcy.org
This organization provides legal representation to low-income children and youth in and around Toronto, Canada.

Juvenile Justice Information Exchange
JJIE Newsroom
Center for Sustainable Journalism
Kennesaw State University
1000 Chastain Road
MD 2212, Building 22, Room 5007B
Kennesaw, GA 30144
Website: http://www.jjie.org
This community-supported information source covers juvenile justice and related issues.

National Center for Juvenile Justice
3700 South Water Street, Suite 200
Pittsburgh, PA 15203
(412) 227-6950
Website: http://www.ncjj.org
A private, not-for-profit organization, the National Center for Juvenile Justice has conducted research into juvenile crime and delinquency since 1973.

National Gang Center
Institute for Intergovernmental Research
P.O. Box 12729
Tallahassee, FL 32317
Website: http://www.nationalgangcenter.gov
This organization is funded by the U.S. Department of Justice and dedicated to providing research and analysis of gang activity and antigang programs.

National Juvenile Defender Center
1350 Connecticut Avenue NW, Suite 304
Washington, DC 20036
(202) 452-0010
Website: http://www.njdc.info
This independent organization is dedicated to improving the access children in the United States have to qualified legal representation.

WEBSITES

Because of the changing nature of Internet links, Rosen Publishing has developed an online list of websites related to the subject of this book. This site is updated regularly. Please use this link to access this list:

http://www.rosenlinks.com/KYR/Court

FOR FURTHER READING

Champion, Dean J. The *Juvenile Justice System: Delinquency, Processing, and the Law. Upper Saddle River,* NJ: Prentice-Hall, 2009.

Chesney-Lind, and Meda and Randall G. Shelden. *Girls, Delinquency, and Juvenile Justice*. Hoboken, NJ: Wiley-Blackwell, 2014.

Christen, Carol, and Richard N. Bolles. *What Color Is Your Parachute? For Teens: Discovering Yourself, Defining Your Future*. Emeryville, CA: Ten Speed Press, 2010.

Cox, Steven M., Jennifer M. Allen, Robert D. Hanser, and John J. Conrad. *Juvenile Justice: A Guide to Theory, Policy, and Practice.* Thousand Oaks, CA: SAGE Publications, 2011.

Dowd, Nancy E. *Justice for Kids: Keeping Kids Out of the Juvenile Justice System*. New York, NY: NYU Press, 2012.

Hess, Karen M., Christine H. Orthmann, and John P. Wright. *Juvenile Justice.* Independence, KY: Cengage Learning, 2012.

Hile, Lori. *Gangs* (Teen Issues). Chicago, IL: Heinemann-Raintree, 2012.

Howell, James (Buddy) C. *Gangs in America's Communities.* Thousand Oaks, CA: SAGE Publications, Inc., 2011.

Humes, Edward. *No Matter How Loud I Shout: A Year in the Life of Juvenile Court.* New York, NY: Simon & Schuster, 1997.

Jackson, Lindsay. *101 Things Teens Should Know: A Big Sister's Guide to Staying Out of Trouble and Other Helpful Hints.* Riverside, NJ: Andrews McMeel Publishing, 2002.

Kryger, Leora. *Juvenile Court: A Judge's Guide for Young Adults and Their Parents.* Lanham, MD: The Scarecrow Press, 2009.

Lawrence, Richard A., and Mario L. Hesse. *Juvenile Justice: The Essentials.* Thousand Oaks, CA: SAGE Publications, Inc. 2011.

Marcovitz, Hal. *Gangs* (Essential Issues). Minneapolis, MN: ABDO Publishing, 2010.

Mays, G. Larry, and Rick Ruddell. *Do the Crime, Do the Time: Juvenile Criminals and Adult Justice in the American Court System.* Santa Barbara, CA: Praeger, 2012.

Ruddell, Rick, and Matthew O. Thomas. *Juvenile Corrections.* Regina, Saskatchewan: Newgate Press, 2009.

Shelden, Randall G. *Delinquency and Juvenile Justice in American Society.* Long Grove, IL: Waveland Press, 2011.

Sullivan, Irene. *Raised by the Courts: One Judge's Insight into Juvenile Justice.* New York, NY: Kaplan Trade, 2010.

Taylor, Robert, and Eric Fritsch. *Juvenile Justice: Policies, Programs, and Practices.* New York, NY: McGraw-Hill Humanities, 2010.

Whitehead, John T., and Steven P. Lab. *Juvenile Justice: An Introduction.* Waltham, MA: Anderson Publishing, 2013.

Winn, Maisha T. *Girl Time: Literacy, Justice, and School-to-Prison Pipeline.* New York, NY: Teachers College Press, 2011.

BIBLIOGRAPHY

ABA Collateral Consequences. "Federal." Retrieved March 5, 2014 (http://www.abacollateralconsequences.org/map).

Center on Juvenile and Criminal Justice. "Juvenile Justice History." Retrieved February 19, 2014 (http://www.cjcj.org/Education1/Juvenile-Justice-History.html).

Gately, Gary. "For Juveniles, the Elusive Right to Legal Counsel." Juvenile Justice Information Exchange, November 12, 2013. Retrieved February 19, 2014 (http://jjie.org/for-juveniles-the-elusive-right-to-legal-counsel).

Hockenberry, Sara. "Juveniles in Residential Placement, 2010." Juvenile Offenders and Victims: National Report Series, June 2013. Retrieved February 20, 2014 (http://www.ojjdp.gov/pubs/241060.pdf).

Hockenberry, Sarah, Melissa Sickmund, and Anthony Sladky. "Juvenile Residential Facility Census 2010: Selected Findings." Juvenile Offenders and Victims: National Report Series, September 2013. Retrieved February 19, 2014 (http://www.ojjdp.gov/pubs/241134.pdf).

Human Rights Watch. "The Rest of Their Lives: Life Without Parole for Juvenile Offenders in the United States," October 12, 2005. Retrieved February 19, 2014 (http://www.hrw.org/node/11578/section/1).

Law Office of Thomas P. Hogan, Attorney at Law. "Questionnaire: Choosing a Juvenile Defense Attorney." Retrieved February 27, 2014 (http://www.tomhoganlaw.com/criminal-law/juvenile-justice/questionnaire-choosing-a-juvenile-defense-attorney).

Leverich, Jean. *Juvenile Justice*. Farmington Hills, MI: Greenhaven Press, 2009.

Mays, G. Larry, and Rick Ruddel. *Do the Crime, Do the Time: Juvenile Criminals and Adult Justice in the American Court System*. Santa Barbara, CA: Praeger, 2012.

McCord, Joan, Cathy Spatz Widom, and Nancy A. Crowell. *Juvenile Crime, Juvenile Justice*. Washington, DC: National Academies Press, 2001.

Michon, Kathleen. "Constitutional Rights in Juvenile Cases," Nolo Law for All. Retrieved February 26, 2014 (http://www.nolo.com/legal-encyclopedia/constitutional-rights-juvenile-proceedings-32224.html).

National Gang Center. "National Youth Gang Survey Analysis." Retrieved February 10, 2014 (http://www.nationalgangcenter.gov/Survey-Analysis).

National Juvenile Defender Center. "Minimum Age for Delinquency Adjudication, State Data." Retrieved February 19, 2014 (http://www.njdc.info/state_data_minimum_age.php).

National Juvenile Defender Center. "Waiver of the Right to Counsel." Retrieved February 26, 2014 (http://www.njdc.info/pdf/Waiver_of_the_Right_to_Counsel.pdf).

Nolo Law for All. "Felonies, Misdemeanors, and Infractions: Classifying Crimes." Retrieved February 17, 2014 (http://www.nolo.com/legal-encyclopedia/crimes-felonies-misdemeanors-infractions-classification-33814.html).

Office of the Ohio Public Defender. "Juvenile Rights in the Criminal Justice System." Retrieved February 24, 2014 (http://www.opd.ohio.gov/Juvenile/Jv_Rights.htm).

Offices of the United States Attorneys. "Arrest of a Juvenile." Criminal Resource Manual, United States Attorneys Manual. Retrieved February 25, 2014 (http://www.justice.gov/usao/eousa/foia_reading_room/usam/title9/crm00043.htm).

Puzzanchera, Charles. "Juvenile Arrests 2010." Juvenile Offenders and Victims: National Report Series, December 2013.

Rinehart, William A. *How to Clear Your Adult and Juvenile Criminal Records*. Port Townsend, WA: Loompanics Unlimited, 1997.

Tried as Adults. "Torey's Story – Introduction." Retrieved March 5, 2014 (http://triedasadults.org/story.html).

U.S. Census Bureau. "2010 Census Data." Retrieved February 21, 2014 (http://www.census.gov/2010census/data).

U.S. Department of Health and Human Services. "The truth about having a juvenile record." Girlshealth.gov, Retrieved March 6, 2014 (http://www.girlshealth.gov/future/record/index.html).

U.S. Department of Justice, Office of Juvenile Justice and Delinquency Prevention. Retrieved February 24, 2014 (http://www.ojjdp.gov).

INDEX

ABOUT THE AUTHOR

In over two decades of business experience, Richard Barrington has a working knowledge of legal issues ranging from drafting and reviewing contracts to enforcing employment agreements. More recently, he has written a biography of Supreme Court Justice Sonia Sotomayor. Barrington is also a senior financial analyst for MoneyRates.com and has written for a variety of websites on subjects including personal finance, employment, and education. His articles have been syndicated on MSN.com, the Huffington Post, and Forbes.com, and he has appeared on National Public Radio's *Talk of the Nation* and American Public Media's *Marketplace*. He graduated from St. John Fisher College with a B.A. in Communications and earned his chartered financial analyst designation from the CFA Institute.

ABOUT THE EXPERT REVIEWER

Lindsay A. Lewis, Esq., is a practicing criminal defense attorney in New York City, where she handles a wide range of matters, from those discussed in this series to high-profile federal criminal cases. She believes that each and every defendant deserves a vigorous and informed defense. Ms. Lewis is a graduate of the Benjamin N. Cardozo School of Law and Vassar College.

PHOTO CREDITS

Cover Lisa F. Young/Shutterstock.com (figures), Junial Enterprises/Shutterstock.com (courtroom); cover (background), p. 1 Christophe Rolland/Shutterstock.com; pp. 5, 9, 28, 41 © AP Images; p. 13 © Marmaduke St. John/Alamy; p. 16 Yellow Dog Productions/The Image Bank/Getty Images; p. 17 Mike Fiala/Hulton Archive/Getty Images; p. 19 Monkey Business Images/Shutterstock.com; p. 21 David Young-Wolff/The Image Bank/Getty Images; p. 23 John Suchocki/The Republican/Landov; p. 25 Lihee Avidan/Photonica World/Getty Images; p. 31 Rich Legg/E+/Getty Images; p. 33 © iStockphoto.com/ImagesbyTrista; p. 37 Lou Jones/The Image Bank/Getty Images; p. 39 Chuck Liddy/MCT/Landov; p. 42 © Catchlight Visuals Services/Alamy; p. 43 Goodluz/Shutterstock.com; p. 45 AlexRaths/iStock/Thinkstock; p. 48 moodboard/SuperStock.

Designer: Brian Garvey; Editor: Christine Poolos